W9-COM-568

Claire's Holiday Adventures

Life, Liberty, and the Pursuit of Jellybeans

A Fourth of July Story

Written and Illustrated by Heather French Henry

Cubbie Blue Publishing
Woodland Hills, California

Design by Jaye Oliver

Published by Cubbie Blue Publishing
21900 Marylee Street, #290, Woodland Hills, CA 91367

Printed in the United States of America

Publisher's Cataloging-in-Publication Data

Henry, Heather French.

   Life, liberty, and the pursuit of jellybeans : a Fourth of July story / written and illustrated by Heather French Henry. -- Woodland Hills, CA : Cubbie Blue Publishing, 2004.

      p. ; cm.
      (Claire's holiday adventures)

      Audience: ages 4-10.
      Summary: Claire learns from Ben Franklin and the founding fathers that the Fourth of July is more than fireworks; it's the celebration of our basic freedoms.

      ISBN: 0-9706341-6-1
      0-9706341-5-3 (book with CD)
      1-932824-00-6 (pbk.)

      1. Fourth of July--Juvenile fiction. 2. United States--History-- Juvenile fiction. 3. Liberty--Juvenile fiction. I. Title. II. Series.

PZ7.H467 L54 2004   2003114800
[E]--dc22   0407

10 9 8 7 6 5 4 3 2 1

"I want jellybeans now," insisted Claire, after breakfast.

"It's too early for candy," Mom answered. "It's the Fourth of July. You can have some at the fireworks tonight."

"You don't give me any freedom," yelled Claire. "I'm going to play with Robbie. He lets me do what I want." She ran outside with her puppy, Pepper, in her arms.

Claire couldn't find Robbie but was glad to see her neighbor at the picnic table. "Hello, General Jones," she sobbed. "I'm unhappy."

"What's wrong?" asked the general. "This is the day the patriots signed the Declaration of Independence for 'life, liberty, and the pursuit of happiness.'"

"Independence is freedom, isn't it?" Claire replied.

"Yes, it's the freedom to find happiness," explained General Jones.

Claire stomped her foot. "I don't have freedom. Mom makes all the rules." She buried her face in Pepper's fur.

Her neighbor smiled. "You have to learn how to be free, Claire. Your mom makes good rules. That's what the Declaration of Independence is about—good rules for a free country."

"Freedom!" Robbie yelled, throwing poppers on the ground. Pepper growled.

"The shot heard round the world!" declared General Jones.

"What?" asked Robbie.

"It was the first shot fired in the fight for America's independence from the British."

"Robbie, throw your poppers somewhere else so you don't scare Pepper," demanded Claire, guarding her puppy.

General Jones smiled at his smart little friend. "Good rule, Claire."

"Wow," Mom exclaimed. "What a flash!"

General Jones nodded. "Ben Franklin would have gotten a good jolt."

Robbie scanned the sky. "Ben Franklin signed the Declaration of Independence. Did that give him a jolt?"

"No," Mom laughed. "The jolt came when Franklin flew his kite in a storm and electricity traveled down the kite string . . . Let's duck inside, Claire, before it rains."

"You'd better run home too, Robbie," Mom added.

"But he just got here." Claire frowned and glanced at General Jones.

"Good rules," he whispered.

Claire sighed. "Okay, Mom."

Back home, Claire curled up on her bed with her puppy. "Pepper, do you know why I didn't let Robbie throw poppers near you? Because good rules make us happy. Hmm, I'm almost ready to be free."

The pounding rain had her very sleepy.

Suddenly she heard a voice. "Claire, the patriots need you."
Through her window she saw Benjamin Franklin holding two kites.
He waved. "Come on, Claire. We've got to go work on the
Declaration of Independence."

It turned out he had two kites, which pulled them into the bright sky. As the two floated away, fluffy white clouds tickled Claire's nose, making her squeal with delight. She loved flying through the air with Mr. Franklin.

Looking down, Claire saw barns, churches, and people of all ages.
Then she spotted British soldiers marching down a road with their guns.
Patriots crouched behind trees and rocks.

Robbie, hiding behind a tree, waved up at her. "Look! Robbie's a patriot," she exclaimed.

Before any shots were fired, the wind caught the kites and the two sailed away.

Claire and Ben landed beside a white house. "Where are we?" asked Claire. "I'm starting to miss my puppy."

"We're in Philadelphia," said Ben. "I'll sign the Declaration of Independence then get you home."

They walked into a room with lots of books and a big globe. Four men were at a table studying a large sheet of paper. Claire sat on the floor next to the globe.

Ben made the change and signed the document. "Time for us to go," he said.

The men waved good-bye. "Thank you, Claire," they called. "Come back quickly, Ben. We have to get to Congress to vote for freedom."

"I'll be back in a flash," he yelled.

This time as Claire and Ben floated over towns and farms, it began to pour. Not wanting lightning to hit their kites, the two let go of them and sailed through the storm with their arms and legs stretched wide.

They landed softly, along with their kites, in Claire's yard. Ben shook her hand and said, "Thank you."

"You're welcome, Ben. You'd better hurry back for the vote." While watching him float away, Claire closed her eyes and grinned.

"Claire, wake up," said Mom.

The eight year old sat up with a start. "What a day, Mom! First I learned about rules for freedom, from General Jones. Then I flew to Philadelphia with Mr. Franklin and helped with everyone's freedom."

"Mom," she added, "I think Robbie and I should have jellybeans at the fireworks tonight."

Mom hugged her. "I agree."

Pepper wagged her tail and barked.

A Brief History of the Fourth of July

In the early 1770s, the thirteen colonies along North America's eastern seaboard were ruled by Great Britain. The "mother country" made all the laws and imposed taxes on its "children." But the colonists had no representatives in the British Parliament to speak for their interests.

In December 1773, colonists in Boston, Massachusetts, rebelled by dumping tea into the harbor. Other colonists began gathering military supplies and calling themselves patriots. In April 1775, British troops fought patriots in Lexington, Massachusetts, a battle starting with "the shot heard round the world." Fighting broke out also in nearby Concord. Representatives from all thirteen colonies then met at the Continental Congress, in Philadelphia, Pennsylvania, and made George Washington commander of the American Army.

In June 1776, Congress selected a committee of five to prepare a declaration of independence from British rule. Thomas Jefferson wrote the first draft in secret, penning the phrase "all men are created equal." On July 2, 1776, Congress voted to become independent of Great Britain. On July 4, 1776, Congress officially adopted the Declaration of Independence. And ever since, the Fourth of July has been called Independence Day.

The Declaration of Independence is considered the most important statement of our country's ideas. The original parchment copy, signed by representatives from all the colonies in August 1776, is on display at the National Archives in Washington, DC.

Picture HENRY

Henry, Heather French.

Life, liberty, and the pursuit of jellybeans

pursuit of jellybeans :

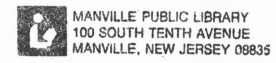
DEMCO